The Purrfect Sleepover

Lucy Daniels

STORY ONE:
Cat Sitters

HO/CH

The Purrfect Sleepover

With special thanks to Janet Bingham
For Jack and Scarlett

ORCHARD BOOKS

First published in Great Britain in 2018 by The Watts Publishing Group

1 3 5 7 9 10 8 6 4 2

Text copyright © Working Partners Limited, 2018
Illustrations copyright © Working Partners Limited, 2018

A CIP catalogue record for this book
is available from the British Library.

ISBN 978 1 40835 400 1

Printed and bound in Great Britain by CPI Group (UK) Ltd, Croydon, CR0 4YY

The paper and board used in this book are made from wood from responsible sources.

Orchard Books
An imprint of
Hachette Children's Group
Part of The Watts Publishing Group Limited
Carmelite House
50 Victoria Embankment
London EC4Y 0DZ

An Hachette UK Company
www.hachette.co.uk
www.hachettechildrens.co.uk

STORY TWO:
Caturday!

STORY ONE:
Cat Sitters

CHAPTER ONE

Amelia Haywood rocked from foot to foot, watching anxiously as Mr and Mrs Hope examined Star. The tortoiseshell kitten was lying on the examination table at the Animal Ark veterinary surgery. Star was just waking up from an anaesthetic, and she was floppy, her golden eyes half-closed. The tip of her little pink tongue stuck out.

Amelia glanced up at the two vets nervously. They were still wearing their green scrubs and plastic medical gloves.

"Star is fine, Amelia," said Mrs Hope, as calm and efficient as ever. "She's sleepy from the operation, but it went well." The vet pointed to the bare patch on Star's tummy. It had been shaved, and a bright red line was stitched across her pink and black-spotted skin.

Amelia let out a breath of relief. She'd been worried about the operation at first, even though Mr and Mrs Hope had explained it was very straightforward and the best thing for Star. Without the procedure, there was a risk that Star would have kittens of her own when she was fully grown. Amelia wanted to be a responsible pet owner, so she had arranged the spaying operation as soon as her kitten was old enough.

Amelia stroked the black and ginger patches, flecked with white, on Star's back. She still remembered the day that she and her best friend Sam had found the kittens at his parents' Bed and

Breakfast. Their mother, a stray called Caramel, had given birth to her babies in the garage!

"Neat stitches!" said Sam. He loved animals almost as much as Amelia did. Being official helpers at Animal Ark was a dream come true for both of them. The vet's surgery was Amelia's favourite place in the whole of Welford.

Mr Hope chuckled. "Thank you, Sam. I'm proud of my needlework! The stitches will dissolve eventually, and Star's fur will grow back quickly."

"What's that strange film over her

eyes?" asked Amelia.

"They're her third eyelids," said Mrs Hope. "Cats have an extra membrane to spread tears and help protect the front of their eyes. Star's will slide back in a few hours, when she wakes up properly. Keep her quiet and let her sleep as long as she likes. She'll soon be feeling better."

Mr Hope passed Amelia a card, with 'Animal Ark Certificate of Feline Vaccinations' written on the front. "Here's the record of Star's jabs," he said. "She won't need another until she has her booster next year. You can take her home now. Just be careful of her tummy."

Amelia gently picked Star up. "How

long will it take until she's healed?"

"Bring her back on Monday so we can look at her stitches," said Mrs Hope. "She'll be a bit sore for a few days. Julia in reception will give you a leaflet on aftercare."

"Can she go outside soon?" asked Amelia. She was desperate to show Star the garden, but kittens couldn't go outdoors until they'd had their vaccinations and were old enough.

"Best keep her indoors for at least another week," said Mrs. Hope. "But by next weekend she'll be ready to explore the great outdoors."

Amelia was glad it was the half-term

holiday soon, so she would be at home to look after Star. "Do you hear that, Star?" she whispered. "You're going to go outside soon. Want to come over the first time she goes out, Sam?"

"I wouldn't miss it," he replied. "Neither would Mac."

"By the way," said Mrs Hope, "we've got a visitor coming over next Saturday. An old friend from veterinary college called Rosemary Lo. She's a cat expert. I'm sure she'd love to meet you both!"

Amelia grinned. *A cat expert – what a cool job!*

"We're thinking of hosting a special day here at the surgery, with a focus on felines," said Mr Hope. "Care advice, diet, behaviour – the complete picture for cat owners."

Amelia had an idea. "You could call it Caturday!" she said excitedly.

Sam high-fived her.

Mrs Hope clapped her hands. "Caturday! I love it."

"Me too," said Mr Hope.

Amelia beamed. *This is another chance for us to prove ourselves!* she thought.

"We're doing the Ancient Egyptians at school," said Sam. "They really loved cats. We could make an exhibition about it!"

"Oh, yes!" said Amelia. "There are information sheets in our classroom. I bet Miss Hafiz will let us bring them in."

"Brilliant," said Mr Hope. "I can see you're just the pair to make Caturday a success. We'll ask Julia to put something on the Animal Ark website."

Sam's eyes were dancing. "This is so exciting!" he said.

Amelia nodded. *I can't wait!*

Amelia's mum drove them home. The
phone started ringing as she opened the
front door. Gran was at her Pilates class,
so Amelia's mum ran to answer it.
"Hello?" she said. "Oh hi, Sue. How are
you?" She frowned as she listened. "Of
course. Don't worry. We'll take good care
of Luna."

Amelia and Sam exchanged glances.
Luna was a kitten who belonged to Ellie
Wright in the year below them. She
lived a few doors down. *I wonder what's
wrong ...*

Mum put the phone down. "That was

Ellie's mum. Ellie's granddad is poorly, so they've all gone to visit him. They won't be back till tomorrow. Mrs Wright asked if you'd feed Luna and play with her so she doesn't get lonely."

"Of course," said Amelia. "I'll just get Star settled first."

Very gently, Amelia lifted Star out of the travel basket. The third eyelids were shrinking down into the corners of her eyes, and the tip of her tongue had disappeared back into her mouth.

"She's looking better," Sam said.

"But she's shivering," said Amelia. "Can she have a hot water bottle please, Mum?"

Mum gave her the bottle and a towel

to wrap around it, and Amelia carefully tucked it next to Star in her basket. The kitten gave a weak purr before closing her eyes again. Amelia stroked Star's ears. "I'm going to go and see Luna now," she told her kitten. "She needs my help, but I'll be back soon."

"I'll come too if you like," said Sam.

Amelia and Sam let themselves into Ellie's house with the spare key Mum kept for emergencies. Luna came running to meet them as soon as the key rattled in the door.

She was a fluffy kitten, a bit older than Star, with grey fur and blue eyes. Amelia had seen her making her way across their back garden a couple of times. Luna wound around their ankles, tail up and purring. Amelia sat on the hall floor and Luna climbed on to her lap and head-butted her under the chin.

Sam sat down next to her and
stroked Luna's fur. "She has really pretty
markings."

Amelia gently tipped Luna off her
knee. "Come on, kitty. Let's find some
food for you."

They wandered into the kitchen. Ellie's
mum had left some sachets of food out
on the kitchen worktop. Luna stretched

up Amelia's legs, watching her empty one into a bowl and chop up the meat.

Sam picked up another dish. "I'll get her some fresh water."

They put the bowls on the floor. Luna took a few bites of food and lapped up a little water, before padding towards her cat flap.

Amelia chuckled. "She's more interested in playing outside than eating."

They unlocked the back door and went out into the garden. The patio was cluttered with bikes, plants and garden furniture, and there was a stuffed mouse lying under a chair. Sam threw it, and Luna dashed away and brought it back, dropping it at his feet. Sam laughed, making his black curls bounce. "She can retrieve better than Mac, and he's a puppy!"

After half an hour of fetching toys and pouncing on sticks that Amelia and Sam wiggled on the ground, Luna sat down and began to wash. She licked her paw and circled it past her ear and down over the side of her face a few times. Then she started on the other side with the same slow, neat movements.

"I think she's getting tired at last," said Amelia.

"Phew!" said Sam. "I know I am!"

Luna followed them inside and jumped into her basket as Amelia locked the back door. The tabby kitten was purring contentedly as they left.

"She's falling asleep," whispered Amelia.

"All that playing has tired her out," said Sam. "Cat sitting is easy!"

Amelia nodded and grinned. "Easy, and fun too!"

CHAPTER TWO

"Star! Star! Where are you?" Amelia
padded across the moonlit park in
her fluffy slippers. Star was out here
somewhere, lost and frightened. The
thorns on the bushes caught on Amelia's
pyjama legs. She pulled free and called
for Star again. She searched and searched,

but there was no sign of her kitten. A yowl rang out in the darkness. Amelia shivered with worry. *Star!*

Amelia woke up with a start, goose pimples racing over her skin. She rolled over and breathed a sigh of relief. Star was safe in her basket beside the bed.

Thank goodness it was just a dream!

A cat yowled again. But this time it was real and coming from somewhere outside. Amelia jumped out of bed and ran to the little seat under her bedroom window. In the distance she saw the silhouette of Sam's house, the B&B's waterwheel curving against the skyline. Amelia pressed her nose to the window, peering out into the dark night. The cat yowled again, and then another cat let out a loud screech, but Amelia couldn't tell exactly where the noises were coming from.

Star left her basket and climbed on to Amelia's lap. Her ears twitched nervously. Amelia cuddled her reassuringly. "It's all right, Star. It's a cat fight, but they can't hurt you." She took one last look out into the darkness. "I just hope they don't hurt each other. And I really hope one of them isn't Luna!"

The next morning, Amelia and Sam went straight to Ellie's house to check on Luna. Sam had Mac on his lead, and

he waited outside with the Westie puppy
while Amelia went in. She waited in the
hall, rattling the key and calling, "Luna!
Here, kitty! Where are you?"

But no kitten came running this time.

Where is she? thought Amelia.

She went along the hall, still calling.
The kitchen was empty. Amelia's heart
sank when she saw the feeding bowls.
Yesterday's leftover meat was still there,
dried up in the dish.

She ran back to the front door. "Sam!
She isn't here! We have to find her."

Sam gave Mac a gentle tug, pulling
the puppy away from the hedge he was
sniffing. "Maybe she's inside somewhere."

They searched downstairs first, looking under the sofa and all the chairs in the sitting room. Sam peered behind the curtains and gave them a shake, but there was no sign of the kitten. They searched the cloakroom and Amelia even checked the washing machine in the kitchen, just in case the cat had somehow managed to crawl inside. *Oh, Luna … Where have you got to?*

"Let's try upstairs," said Sam. Mac bounded up ahead of them. Ellie's room was very tidy, and Amelia's heart leapt when she saw something grey and fluffy curled up on her pillow. Then she realised that it was only a stuffed toy.

After they'd searched Ellie's bedroom, they looked in a messy room with bunk beds. But Luna wasn't in there. She wasn't in the bathroom either, or in Ellie's parents' bedroom. Mac found a dusty tartan slipper under the big bed, but no Luna.

"It's hopeless," Amelia groaned. "She's not here."

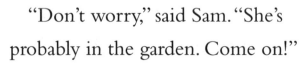

"Don't worry," said Sam. "She's probably in the garden. Come on!"

Ellie's garden had a neatly mown lawn beyond the patio, with a rope swing hanging from a cherry tree at the end of the grass.

Amelia and Sam began their search on the patio. Mac followed them around, sniffing at the bikes and flower pots. When Sam peered under a bushy plant, Mac lay down and looked there too. When Sam shifted a loose coil of hosepipe, Mac pounced on it and gave it a shake.

Amelia's chest got tighter with worry every minute. At last, she flopped down on a white plastic chair. "This is awful, Sam. We're supposed to be looking after Luna, not losing her!"

Sam fist-bumped her shoulder. "Hey! Don't give up. I know – maybe Mac can sniff her out!" He picked up one of Luna's garden toys and held it out to Mac. "Here, Mac. This is Luna's smell. Where is she, boy?"

Mac gave the toy a sniff, and a lick for good measure, then padded around the garden.

"Yip!" Mac jumped up at the cherry tree, resting his front paws on the smooth brown trunk. "Yip!"

"He's found her!" cried Sam.

Amelia peered up into the branches and gave a sigh of relief. "Luna!" she whispered. "There you are!" The tabby kitten was crouched, shivering, on a branch. But something was wrong. Her fur was matted into damp tufts, and her eyes were huge. The black pupils in the middle were so wide and round that only a thin circle of blue showed around them.

The cat let out a sad meow.

Amelia kept her voice soft and low. "Don't worry, Luna. We'll get you down."

Sam brought over a plastic garden

chair. Amelia stood
on it and reached up
for the kitten. "Come
on, Luna," she coaxed.
"Don't be frightened."

Luna seemed to
remember that Amelia
was a friend. With
another anxious meow,
the kitten edged along
the branch and let
Amelia pick her up.

Amelia passed her to Sam and climbed down from the chair.

She could see straight away that there was a deep scratch and a missing patch of fur on Luna's head. And when Amelia ran her hands over the kitten's body, she felt Luna flinch. Amelia's stomach knotted anxiously. "She's got scratches

all over. I think she was in the cat fight I heard last night. She must have hidden in the tree to escape the other cat." Amelia looked up at Sam. "We need to get her to Animal Ark straight away!"

CHAPTER THREE

Once again, Amelia found herself
watching anxiously as Mr and Mrs
Hope examined a kitten. But this time
it wasn't Star – it was Luna. The vets
ran their hands over her, checking
every inch of her body. Luna's legs were
quivering with fear. Amelia was sure she

would take any chance to leap off the examination table and run away.

Mrs Hope rubbed Luna's ears reassuringly. "Poor Luna. She's been in quite a fight. These are definitely cat scratches, and she's been badly frightened."

"Will she be all right?" asked Amelia, the knot in her stomach twisting. She felt really guilty that Luna had been injured when she was looking after her.

"Oh, yes," Mr Hope said. "She'll be sore and nervous for a while, but she'll soon be right as rain. Luna will need antibiotics to stop the scratches becoming infected, though. I'll just call Ellie's parents." He went out to the reception area.

"I feel really bad that Luna got hurt," Amelia said quietly. "Do you think Ellie and her parents will be angry with me?"

"It's not your fault," said Mrs Hope. "Unless they're locked up indoors all the time, cats do get into scrapes. It would have happened even if the Wrights had been at home."

Amelia felt the knot in her stomach loosen a little.

Mr Hope soon came back into the examination room. "That's all fine. Mr Wright says they'll be home later today."

Amelia gave him a grateful smile. "Ellie must be desperate to see poor Luna now that she knows she's hurt."

Mr and Mrs Hope gave Luna pain relief and antibiotic injections, and put her back in her cat travel-basket.

Amelia and Sam were just collecting Mac from the reception area, when a dark-haired boy came in carrying a stack of papers. Amelia recognised him from the year above at school, but she wasn't sure of his name.

"Hi, Julia," the boy said to the receptionist. "Look at the posters I made! Can I put some up in here?"

Peering over, Amelia saw that the posters were decorated with cat cartoons and bright lettering.

CATURDAY!

A day of feline fun brought to you by Animal Ark.

Learn all about cat care, cat facts and cat history!

Special Guest: cat expert Dr Rosemary Lo.
THIS SATURDAY AT ANIMAL ARK!!

Amelia and Sam frowned at each other.

"Very nice, Tarik," Julia said, wheeling over to get a closer look.

Amelia blurted, "Are you helping out at Caturday too?"

The boy gave her a wide grin. "Of course! I can't wait for Saturday. Or should I say *Caturday*! I'm Tarik, by the way. You're the new girl at school, aren't you? Olivia, right?"

"Amelia," Sam corrected him. "And I'm Sam. "

"Oh, sorry. Isn't Caturday a great idea?"

"Yes," said Sam. "Actually, it was Amelia who thought of it."

Tarik looked surprised. "Really? That's

cool. I had to bring my cat in last night for his flea treatment and the Hopes told me all about it." He tapped the poster and chuckled. "I feel like *I* could give a talk about cats myself – I've been in this place so many times over the years."

He paused to take a breath, and Amelia leapt in. "Do the Hopes know you've made the posters?"

Tarik nodded. "I showed them the design this morning. They were surprised, but really pleased." He held two of the posters out. "Here, take a couple to put up at home. Are you both coming on Saturday?"

Bristling, Amelia took the poster automatically. *Of course we're coming*, she thought, annoyed. But she didn't say anything.

"Thanks, Tarik," said Sam. "We'll see you there." He gave Amelia's sleeve a tug and pulled her towards the door.

Amelia chewed her lip as they walked home. Finally she burst out, "Didn't you think that was weird? He was a bit … bossy, wasn't he?"

"Tarik?" said Sam. "I think he's just enthusiastic."

Amelia could feel herself getting angry. "Who does he think he is? We're the ones who help out at Animal Ark, not him. And Caturday was *my* idea. We should be the ones making posters!"

Sam shrugged. "It's good to have extra help, isn't it? And they're brilliant posters!"

Deep down, Amelia knew that Sam was right. Tarik was just being helpful.

She sighed. *But what if the Hopes like him more than us? He might get to help out at Animal Ark instead of us!*

Sam seemed to read her mind. "Don't worry. We'll think of something else to do to help. Something even better."

Back at Ellie's house, Sam shut Mac in the living room with a chew toy, then he and Amelia took Luna into the kitchen. Amelia opened the lid of the cat basket. The kitten was crouched in the corner, trembling.

Amelia coaxed her gently. "Come on, Luna. You're safe at home now."

Luna slowly uncurled herself and peeped over the top of the basket.

Amelia lifted her out.
They put down bowls
of fresh food and water,
and Luna lapped a
little before wandering
around the kitchen,
sniffing everything and
peering round corners.

Amelia and Sam sat
on the floor, waiting patiently. At last
Luna came over to them and head-
butted their knees. Amelia stroked her
head. "Good girl, Luna. You know you're
home now, don't you?"

"Let's take her into the garden to play,"
Sam suggested.

They opened the back door, but Luna stayed put.

"She's worried," said Sam.

Amelia nodded. "She must be scared the other cat will come back."

"It's OK, Luna," said Sam.

At last Luna stood up, stretched and padded outside. She found her stuffed mouse on the patio and swiped at it. Then she pounced and rolled over, clutching the mouse to her chest, chewing it and purring.

"Phew!" said Amelia. "Thank goodness, she's relaxed at last!"

Suddenly a movement out in the garden caught Amelia's eye. She gasped.

A huge ginger tom cat sat on the fence. He had a pale scar across his nose, his tail was crooked and the edges of his ears were frayed as though from fighting.

"Oh, no. Sam, look!"

"Uh-oh!" muttered Sam. "He looks tough!"

The ginger cat scanned the garden

with his orange eyes. Then he saw Luna.

"*Hiisss!!!*" The tom arched his back and a ridge of fur stood up along his spine. His tail pointed to the sky, bristling like a bottle brush. Amelia flinched. Then the ginger cat leapt down from the fence and hurtled straight towards Luna!

CHAPTER FOUR

"*YOWL!!*"

The ginger cat pounced, claws out.
Luna spat, her ears flattened back against
her head. Then she bolted. The tom cat
twisted in mid-air to follow her. Luna's
fluffed-up tail looked twice its normal
size as she raced for the cherry tree.

In two leaps, she was climbing the trunk, but her attacker was close behind.

Amelia and Sam dashed out on to the patio, but there was no way they could catch the cats.

"What can we do?" Sam asked desperately.

Amelia looked around wildly. "We need something to break up the fight." Then she spotted it. "The hosepipe!"

Sam dived for the

garden tap, and Amelia grabbed the hose.
It lurched as the water began to run.
Amelia yanked the nozzle, pointing it at
the cherry tree. Luna had disappeared into
the leafy branches, and the ginger cat was
halfway up the trunk in hot pursuit. In a
moment he would be hidden and they
wouldn't be able to stop him.

Amelia aimed the nozzle, and the

hosepipe burst into
life. A stream of
water gushed out,
drenching the
ginger cat as it
clung to the tree
trunk's bark.

"Good shot!" yelled Sam.

"*Yowl!*" The tom sprang down, landing in a puddle at the base of the trunk. He suddenly looked much smaller with his wet fur plastered against his body. The ginger cat shook himself and leaped up on the fence. For a moment he teetered there, dripping, before jumping down into the garden on the other side.

"Phew!" said Amelia, as Sam turned off the water. "Quick! Let's get Luna."

The garden chair was still standing by the tree trunk. Amelia stood on it again to reach Luna. This time the grey kitten hung on to the branch with her claws, and Amelia had to prise her free.

She handed Luna down
to Sam, the kitten kicking and
swiping at them.

"Ouch!" Sam stuck his finger in his
mouth. "I'm not that ginger cat, Luna.
Don't scratch me!"

"Let's get her indoors," Amelia said.
"She's terrified."

Back in the kitchen, Luna struggled
free from Sam's arms and went to cower
in her basket. Amelia reached out to
stroke her.

"*Hissss!*"

Amelia pulled her hand back sharply. "Oh, poor kitty. Don't be scared of us. We're your friends, remember?" She looked at Sam. "Maybe if we sit and chat quietly, she'll start to calm down."

"Let's hope you're right," said Sam glumly.

They were still sitting there half an hour later, when Ellie came home. The front door banged open and the Wright family piled noisily into the hall. Luna jumped and hissed again.

"We're in the kitchen," Amelia called out. "Luna's had another fright."

Ellie's mum opened the kitchen door and tiptoed in. "What happened?"

She was followed, less quietly, by Ellie and her five-year old twin brothers, Alfie and Ben. Ellie's dad came in last.

Ellie looked pale and upset. She dropped to her knees by Luna's basket and reached out her hand. The frightened kitten just flinched and gave a sad little meow.

Amelia and Sam quickly explained what had happened. Afterwards, Ellie looked as if she might cry.

"Luna's all right, though, Ellie," said Amelia, giving her a hug. "The other cat didn't catch her this time. She was too fast for him!"

"I'm glad you were here," said Mrs Wright. "Let me guess. Was the other cat big and ginger? Battle-scarred?"

Amelia and Sam nodded mutely, and Ellie's dad sighed. "We know him well. He lives in the house over the back fence."

"Luna's only just started going out, and he chases her every time!" Ellie said.

Just then the kitchen door banged open again. "There's a puppy in the living room!" announced Ben.

"Can we keep him?" asked Alfie.

They all laughed. The twins thundered up the stairs to play, and Mac chased after them, yipping happily.

All the noise made Luna cower in her basket. "Let's leave Luna alone for a while," said Ellie's mum. "Amelia and Sam, why don't you stay for lunch and we'll see how she seems after that?"

But after lunch, Luna still looked frightened. She hissed as Amelia, Ellie and Sam sat down near her basket.

"It's all right," said Ellie. "I just want to stroke you." She reached out a hand.

Luna drew back, lifting one paw.

"Look out!" Amelia warned.

Too late. Luna swatted at Ellie's hand.

"Ouch!" Ellie sucked her finger, eyes wide with shock. "Luna's never scratched me before!"

Luna crept out of her basket and went to sit by the patio door, looking out on to the garden. Ellie tiptoed over and sat down, putting her hand down on the floor. Luna whirled around and bit her finger again.

"OW! Oh, Luna, that really hurt!" Ellie cradled her hand, tears welling up in her eyes. "She's not acting like herself at all!"

Ellie's mum pulled her over to the sink and held her hand under the cold tap. Ellie sniffled. "What's got into her?"

"It's because she's scared," said Amelia.

Mrs Wright sighed. "I'm sure you're right. But I don't know what we can do about it."

"There must be something," said Amelia. "We've got to find a way to help Luna!" She looked at Sam. "We'll try and find out more."

Sam nodded. "I should probably take Mac back home. Come on, Amelia. We can think about it on the walk."

They left Ellie's house and went round the corner. Then they almost bumped into a boy carrying a cardboard box. Amelia was too busy thinking about Luna to take any notice. But then the

66

boy said, "Hello," and her heart sank.

"I hoped I might bump into you," Tarik said. "Look, I saved the last two cupcakes for you!" He flipped the lid off the box. "Aren't they great?"

Amelia blinked at the two cupcakes. They were topped with swirls of icing and decorated like cats' faces. One cat was black and white, and the other had tabby stripes. The cupcakes looked amazing, but Amelia suddenly lost her appetite.

"Did you make them?" asked Sam.

Tarik nodded proudly. "I took them to Animal Ark and gave them to people waiting in reception. Julia ate two!"

Amelia stifled a groan.

"Have you two been letting people know about Caturday too?" Tarik asked.

Amelia sniffed. "We've been busy. We've been helping an injured cat."

Tarik looked impressed. "That's great. Enjoy your cakes. See you at Caturday!"

Sam bit into his cake as Tarik walked away. "These are really good! Try yours, Amelia."

Amelia scowled at her cupcake,

feeling miserable. *Cupcakes ... Why didn't we think of that?* She shook herself, annoyed to be feeling so cross with Tarik, who was only being helpful. Reluctantly she nibbled at the cake. She hated to admit it, but it tasted as good as it looked. Amelia glanced up and saw Tarik let himself into one of the houses across the road.

"Sam!" Amelia grabbed his sleeve and gave him a little shake. "That house ... it backs on to Ellie's. That means ..."

Sam gasped. "Tarik owns the ginger cat that attacked Luna!"

CHAPTER FIVE

Amelia and Sam stared at each other.

"I suppose we'll have to tell Tarik," Sam said.

Amelia nodded. "Of course! He needs to know how mean his cat is being."

They marched up Tarik's garden path and knocked on the door. It was opened a few moments later by a dark-haired woman cradling a tiny baby. Her hair was messy and she had dark circles under her eyes, but she smiled kindly.

"Hello. Are you friends of Tarik's?"

"Um, yes," said Amelia. "Can we see him, please?"

"Of course." The woman called up the stairs, "Tarik! Your friends are here!" Tarik's mum turned back to them and said, "He'll be right here."

Amelia leaned in to peek at the bundle in Tarik's mum's arms. The baby had

spiky black hair and long, dark eyelashes.
"Ahhh," Amelia breathed. "Your baby is
so sweet!"

Tarik grunted as he came down the
stairs. "Until Mum puts her down. Then
she starts screaming."

"You were just the same, Tarik," said
his mum, laughing. "You kept all the
neighbours awake when you were a
baby!"

As if on cue, the baby opened her eyes
and started wailing.

"Excuse me, but I need to go and
change a nappy." Tarik's mum hurried
off, leaving Tarik on the doorstep.

"Hi again!" Tarik said. "Did you like

the cupcakes? Do you want to help me make some more?"

Amelia shook her head crossly. "No. We need to talk about your cat."

"You mean Pumpkin?"

Sam chuckled. "That's a brilliant name for him!"

Amelia nudged Sam hard and he stopped laughing. "Did you know he attacked Luna, the kitten who lives in the next street?" said Amelia.

Tarik's smile faded. "That doesn't sound like Pumpkin. He never scratches or bites. Look how cuddly he is …" He disappeared and came back with the big cat in his arms.

Pumpkin rubbed his head against Tarik and rumbled a deep loud purr. He looked much friendlier than the last time Amelia had seen him.

"He wasn't gentle with Luna!" Amelia insisted.

Tarik shrugged. "Well, you know cats," he said. "They like to defend their territory."

Amelia was getting cross. "He was in Ellie's garden. It's Luna's territory."

Tarik frowned. "Cats don't think like that.'

"Well, maybe their owners should!" snapped Amelia. She turned on her heel and strode off up the road.

"Amelia!" Sam called after her. But Amelia didn't reply.

Later that day, Amelia took Star back to Animal Ark.

Mr and Mrs Hope checked the kitten

over carefully. "Her scar's healing," said Mrs Hope. "And her tummy feels good. There's no swelling or infection. She's doing very well."

"So she can go outside soon?" Amelia asked hopefully.

"By the end of the week," said Mr Hope. "We fitted a microchip when she had her operation. Let's just check it's working properly ..." He ran a little electronic scanner over Star's shoulder and gave a satisfied nod.

Star stayed still and didn't complain the whole time she was being examined. When the Hopes gave her the all clear, Amelia picked Star up and cuddled her.

You're so good, Star, thought Amelia. *I'm really proud of you!*

When Amelia went back through the reception room, Julia was talking to a small woman with a neat bob. The receptionist called Amelia over. "Come and meet Dr Lo!"

"The cat expert!" said Amelia.

The woman smiled. "I've heard a lot about you too, Amelia. The Hopes were telling me on the phone all about how helpful you and your friend Sam have been."

Amelia felt herself blushing. "We love it at Animal Ark," she said.

"And you made such lovely posters for

Caturday!" said Dr Lo, pointing to the one on the noticeboard.

Amelia's mood darkened. "Actually, that was a boy called Tarik."

"Gosh! The Hopes are lucky to have so many helpers," said Dr Lo. "What a pretty tortoiseshell kitten you've got there. I love her nose – pink on one side, black on the other."

Amelia felt a tingle of excitement and pushed Tarik and his posters out of her mind. *Dr Lo is the perfect person to help with Luna!* "Can I ask you something about cats, please?" she said.

"Of course," replied Dr Lo.

Amelia quickly explained about Luna and Pumpkin. "Is there a way to stop them fighting?" she asked breathlessly.

Dr Lo nodded. "Things will settle down once the cats get used to each other. But it will take a little while. Cats really don't like change. In the meantime, there are a few things you can do to help avoid fights …"

Amelia listened eagerly as Dr Lo explained what to do. She couldn't wait to tell Ellie!

CHAPTER SIX

The next day, Amelia and Sam rushed round to Ellie's house. Amelia put a large paper bag on the kitchen worktop and grinned as Ellie and her brothers crowded round. When she emptied the bag, she couldn't help laughing at their confused expressions. Eight oranges and

lots of pine cones tumbled out, followed
by two plastic caterpillars that walked
in crooked circles and a stuffed toy fish.
Ben picked up the fish and squeezed it.
It made a nice crinkly sound.

"The toys are for Luna," explained Amelia. "Dr Lo said you should try and keep her indoors more so she doesn't meet Pumpkin very often. The oranges and pine cones are for outside. They'll help stop Pumpkin coming into the garden."

Ellie wrinkled her nose. "Oranges and pine cones? How will they help?"

Sam peeled one of the oranges and gave Alfie and Ben each a piece to eat. "We just need the peel. Dr Lo said cats hate citrus fruits, like oranges and lemons. So, if we put pieces of orange peel in the garden, Pumpkin will smell it and stay away."

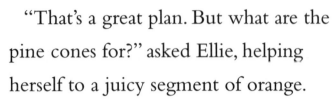

"That's a great plan. But what are the pine cones for?" asked Ellie, helping herself to a juicy segment of orange.

"We can spread them at the bottom of the fence," Amelia explained. "Pumpkin won't want to jump down on them from the fence. They'll look too spiky and wobbly."

"So the big cat will go away again," announced Ben and Amelia nodded.

"Let's do it," said Ellie.

Amelia scooped the orange peel and pine cones into the bag and they all trooped outside. They scattered handfuls of the mixture into the border along the base of the fence.

When the bag was empty, they stood
back to look at all the curls of orange
rind and knobbly pine cones decorating
the flower bed. Sam sniffed. "It smells
like Christmas!"

"And it looks Pumpkin-proof," said
Amelia. "I just hope it works."

"Luna's watching us," said Ellie,
pointing back at the house. Luna was
sitting inside on the windowsill. Her tail
was swishing, so Amelia could tell she
was still cross. It reminded Amelia of
something. *It's not just Luna who's been
getting cross recently …*

"I'm sorry I got angry at Tarik," Amelia
whispered to Sam. "I was being silly."

87

"Don't worry," said Sam. "I get it. Maybe we should try talking to Tarik again. Hopefully we can get him to understand about Pumpkin …"

Just then there was a scrabbling sound and a flash of ginger. Pumpkin appeared on top of the fence. Everyone gasped and waited to see what the big cat would do.

Pumpkin leaned forward on the fence top, swaying slightly. His back legs tensed, ready to jump. Amelia held her breath. Pumpkin hesitated. He saw the pine cones. He sniffed the citrus and rocked back. Then he turned away and jumped back down into his own garden.

"Yay! It worked!" Amelia high-fived Sam and gave Ellie a hug. Ellie's brothers jumped up and down, clapping. Amelia couldn't stop smiling. They had helped Luna today – making the kitten's garden safe for her to play in.

Soon Star will be able to go outside, too … Amelia couldn't wait to show Star the garden. Then she remembered something else, and her smile got even wider.

And it's almost Caturday!

STORY TWO:
Caturday!

CHAPTER ONE

Friday was the last day of the half-term holiday, and Amelia wanted to spend as much time with Star as possible. She gave the kitten her breakfast in the kitchen then ate scrambled eggs with Mum and Gran, watching Star playing all the time. Gran draped her apron over

the back of her chair and Star batted at
the ties, winding them — and herself —
around the chair legs.

"Oh, my goodness," chuckled Gran,
clutching her side. "That kitten is too
cute!"

When she had eaten her eggs, Amelia
reached for some grapes to finish off
her breakfast.

Just then, a sunbeam flickered across the room. Star leapt at it, slipped, and skidded across the floor. Amelia burst out laughing and accidentally dropped a grape. Star pounced, batting at the grape with her paw. A moment later, Amelia, Mum and Gran were all sitting on the floor, rolling grapes for the kitten and giggling as she chased them.

"Everyone in the village is talking about Caturday," said Mum. "Those posters the lad round the corner made are fantastic."

"Hmm," said Amelia. "It wasn't just the posters. Julia did loads of publicity on social media too."

The front doorbell rang.

Sam was waiting on the doorstep with Mac, who had a tennis ball gripped in his jaws. "Hi, Amelia. Want to come for

a walk with us? I bet Mr Stevens hasn't heard about Caturday. He might want to come too."

"Good idea!" said Amelia. Mr Stevens had adopted Star's mother and one of her kittens, to keep the mice off his farm. He probably wouldn't have seen the posters because he was always busy on the farm. And Amelia suspected he didn't use social media.

She bent to pat Mac. His pointed ears twitched and his wagging tail was a blur. They said goodbye to Mum and Gran and set off. Walking past the bus shelter, Amelia noticed one of Tarik's posters stuck on the wall. "They're all over Welford," she grumbled.

Sam gave her a crooked smile. "I saw you'd put one up in your front window."

"Mum put it up. Anyway, I thought we ought to, since he gave them to us."

"Me too. I hung one up in the reception area where our guests will see it. It's good for Animal Ark if lots of people come."

Amelia sighed. "I know. I just don't want the Hopes to think they need him more than they need us."

Sam grinned. "Tarik just wants to help – he's not trying to take over."

They carried on, and soon they reached Mr Stevens's farm. The long, muddy drive had prickly hedgerows bordering the land on either side.

Mac gave a tug on his lead, and Sam

laughed. "Yes, we're going that way, Mac.
When we get to the big field you can
play fetch!"

Suddenly Sam tripped over a rock,
sprawling on his hands and knees. "Ow!"

"Are you OK?" Amelia rushed to help
Sam, but Mac got to him first. Sam sat
in the mud and cuddled the wriggling
puppy. He grinned up at Amelia, shaking
his head.

Amelia held out a hand to help him up, laughing at the muddy streaks on his T-shirt. "You've got paw-prints all over you!"

Sam rubbed himself down and peered at the ground. "I dropped Mac's ball. Did you see where it rolled?"

"Nope," said Amelia, joining the search. A cattle grid stretched across the drive. She stared down at the metal bars.

"Did it fall through one of the gaps?" asked Sam.

Mac approached the edge, keeping his paws off the grid.

"Mac doesn't like it," Amelia said.

Sam nodded. "The cows don't like it

either, because their hooves slip between the gaps. It acts like a gate. Cows won't walk on it, so it keeps them inside on the farm. Oh, I see the ball!" He squatted down and squeezed his hand between the bars, trying to get the tennis ball. "It's no good," he said, shaking his head. "I can't reach."

Amelia knelt down to have a go. The metal bars of the grid dug into her knees and scraped her arm, but she managed to get her fingertips on the ball. Suddenly, a movement caught her eye. The dried leaves gathered in one corner were shifting. Something was rustling them. Amelia frowned. "There's something alive down there …" She peered closer and made out two, then three round objects huddled together. They looked spiky. Her breath caught in her throat and she felt a prickle of goose pimples. "It's hedgehogs! Three baby hedgehogs!"

Sam looked through the grid. "Poor

things!" he whispered. "They must have fallen through the bars." Mac pushed his nose down between the bars at the edge of the grate and whined. "What do you think we should do?"

"We've got to get them out," said Amelia. "Do cattle grids lift up? Maybe Mr Stevens can open it."

Sam nodded. "I'll go up to the farm and try and find him."

"I'll wait here with Mac," said Amelia. "But hurry – we might not have much time!"

Sam sprinted off. A few minutes later, he was back with Mr Stevens in his jeep. The farmer soon had the cattle grid open. Then he took a cardboard box and some thick gloves out of the jeep.

With the grid open, Amelia got a better look at the hedgehog closest to her. Its prickles were tortoiseshell-coloured, tipped with white. She caught a glimpse of its leathery feet, and its tiny heart-shaped face covered in wiry grey and brown hair. The hedgehog's small, beady eyes were dull, and its little pointed nose was dry. Amelia knew that was a bad sign. *Looks like it might be sick!* she thought.

The hedgehog lowered its spines over its face like a hood. It rolled up, tucking itself into a ball of prickles.

Wearing the thick
gloves, Amelia and Sam
carefully placed the
three hedgehogs
in the cardboard
box. When they
had finished,
they looked
up to see Mr
Stevens poking about in the hedgerow.

"I'm afraid I've found their mother,"
said Mr Stevens. He moved a clump of
long grass aside and beckoned them over.
Amelia saw a large hedgehog stretched
out in the hedgerow. It wasn't moving.
"I'm sorry, kids," said Mr Stevens. "It

looks like these little hedgehogs are orphans."

"Oh, no!" Amelia's heart dropped, and she met Sam's eyes. *The poor babies!*

"Let's get them to Animal Ark now," said Mr Stevens. "I've already called to say we're coming."

Amelia and Sam helped Mr Stevens move the cattle grid back into place. Then Sam climbed into the jeep's front seat with Mac at his feet. Mr Stevens pushed aside an assortment of spades, forks and hoes so that Amelia could squeeze into the back seat with the hedgehogs' box beside her.

As the jeep rattled down the country

lane, the hedgehog babies stayed tightly rolled up.

"Hang on, babies," Amelia whispered to them. "We'll soon be at Animal Ark." She felt terrible that they hadn't been able to save their mother. *But we'll save you, little ones. I promise.*

CHAPTER TWO

A few minutes later, Mr Stevens swung the jeep into the little car park at the front of the surgery. Amelia jumped out with the box of hedgehogs. Mr Hope came down the steps to meet them and ushered Amelia and Sam through the front door.

"I'm afraid I have to dash off," said Mr
Stevens. "I hope the little fellows get on
OK. Let me know!"

Mrs Hope was waiting in the
overnight room. She had set up a little
pen on a table, and Amelia saw that there
was a heat mat and bedding inside it.

"Come in," Mrs Hope said. "Pop them in the pen to get warmed up, then we'll start feeding them."

Still wearing the gloves, Amelia and Sam lifted the babies out one at a time and put them on the soft towelling. Amelia could feel the warmth of the heat mat underneath.

"You can help me mix some formula milk for them, like you did for Caramel's litter," said Mrs Hope. "Kitten formula is fine for hoglets too."

Amelia smiled. *Hoglets! That's so cute!*

After they'd mixed the powdered formula with water, they drew the liquid up into three tiny syringes. Mrs Hope gently wrapped one of the hoglets in a towel and held it on her knee. She worked the tip of the syringe into the corner of the hoglet's mouth. Amelia and Sam crowded close to watch.

"There," said Mrs Hope. "Do you see his two little bottom teeth? They come up at around three weeks old. I'd say these hoglets are about three or four weeks old."

Mrs Hope passed the towel-wrapped bundle to Amelia. "Be careful of the spines," she said. "They're already quite sharp."

Amelia pushed the tip of the syringe into the corner of the hoglet's mouth. His black nose twitched, and he chomped his jaws as if he didn't like it. But then Amelia saw his strong pink tongue poke

out, and the little animal swallowed.

"Wow!" breathed Sam.

Mr and Mrs Hope got the other two hoglets feeding, then Mr Hope passed the one he was nursing to Sam. They all sat in a circle, and Amelia smiled at Sam's blissful expression. She knew exactly how he felt. *Feeding hoglets is brilliant!* she thought.

"They're clearly very hungry," said Mr Hope. "It looks like you rescued them just in time."

"How often do they need feeding?" asked Amelia.

"Every two hours at first," said Mrs Hope. "But in a few days, we'll start mixing a little cat food in with the formula, and leave it in their pen for them. They should be able to feed by themselves pretty quickly if we can help them survive the next few days."

We will! thought Amelia, determined that the hoglets would live.

As they were putting the sleepy hoglets back on to their heat mat, Amelia

noticed a thin black and white cat in one of the pens against the wall. She was feeding a newborn black kitten. The kitten was tiny, its ears still flat to its head and its eyes closed.

"Is there just one?" asked Amelia.

Mr Hope nodded. "Yes. The rest of the litter died."

Amelia swallowed, a lump in her throat. "Oh, that's so sad!"

"Yes. But hopefully this one will be all right. We're keeping them both here until the mother is strong enough to go home."

The mother cat stretched and began to wash her tiny baby. She purred

rhythmically as she stroked her rough
pink tongue all over the kitten's face
and body.

"She's a very good mother," said Mrs
Hope.

"Poor thing," said Amelia, "she must
really miss her other kittens."

All of a sudden, Amelia felt sadder than
ever. *I wish the hoglets had someone to love
them like that!*

Next morning, Amelia woke up early
and saw Star still fast asleep in her basket.
She stroked the kitten gently. "Wake up,
Star – it's Caturday! I wish you could
come to Animal Ark too!"

Half an hour later, Amelia and Sam
were waiting on the steps of the surgery
as Julia wheeled over to unlock the
door. Amelia glanced over at Tarik's
poster hanging in the window. She had
to admit it looked good. *I just wish we'd
made them, not Tarik!* she thought.

"Hello, you two," the receptionist said.
"You're bright and early this morning!

Dr Lo won't be here for another hour!"

"Happy Caturday, Julia!" Amelia said. "We've come to help get everything ready." She and Sam lifted the bag they were holding. "We've brought the stuff from school about Ancient Egypt. What should we do first?"

Julia soon put them to work. First they arranged the Ancient Egypt display in the reception area. Miss Hafiz had lent them a statue of Bastet, the cat goddess. The black china cat with its jewelled collar, gold earrings and nose ring looked stunning in the middle of the table.

 Sam put out cups and jugs of juice on another table, and Amelia added a plate of Gran's gingerbread cats.

Next they hung up the Hopes' information posters. There was one about the different breeds of cats, with dozens of pictures of cats in all shapes, sizes and colours. Another poster told about caring for new kittens. A third explained about the body language cats use to communicate. One fact caught Amelia's eye.

"Look, Sam. Sometimes Star blinks at me slowly, as if she's saying 'hello'. It says

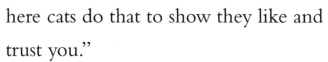

here cats do that to show they like and trust you."

"Makes sense, I suppose," said Sam with a grin. "You wouldn't close your eyes if you thought someone was going to hit you ..." Sam shut his eyes.

Amelia fist-bumped his arm.

"Ouch!" Sam staggered and gave a mock groan. "I knew I couldn't trust you ..."

"Hey, you two!" Julia interrupted them. "Stop goofing around and put these chairs in rows."

They had just finished setting up when the door swung open and Mrs Cranbourne, their elderly friend, walked in. "Hello," she said. "Am I too early?"

"Not at all, Mrs Cranbourne," said Julia. "Everyone will be here soon."

"How is Miss Fizz?" Amelia asked.

Mrs Cranbourne's wrinkled face crinkled into a big, wide smile. "She's very well. I'm looking forward to learning how to care for her even better today."

Dr Lo was next to arrive. She smiled broadly as she admired the displays. "You've all been very busy."

Finally, Mr and Mrs Hope arrived. They looked different today, in casual trousers and T-shirts instead of the green scrubs that they usually wore to work.

"I see our young helpers have been hard at work," said Mrs Hope, beaming at Amelia and Sam.

Soon other people began to arrive, crowding in to take their seats. Amelia grinned at Sam. It looked like Caturday was going to be a success!

CHAPTER THREE

Once everyone was seated, Mrs Hope said, "Welcome, and thank you so much for coming to our special cat day at Animal Ark. We have lots of interesting talks lined up for you. Feel free to ask questions at any time. To kick off, I'd like to talk about the best food to feed your

cat or kitten. Does anybody know how to check your cat is a healthy weight?"

Nobody answered, so Amelia put up her hand. "You should be able to feel its ribs."

Mrs Hope gave her a big smile. "That's right, Amelia." She carried on with her talk and suddenly hands shot up everywhere in the audience as people thought of questions to ask.

Amelia looked around and frowned. "Tarik's not here!" she whispered to Sam.

Her friend's eyebrows went up. "That's odd. He was looking forward to Caturday."

A while later, Mr Hope said, "Time for

a break, everybody. Please help yourself to a cup of tea or squash. Our next talk will be a presentation about big cats given by Scarlett Reed, who works at the safari park."

Everybody crowded around the refreshment table, talking noisily. Mr Hope beckoned to Amelia and Sam. "Hey, guys – I've got a special job for you both.'

They followed him into the calm of the residential unit, or the 'hotel' as it was nicknamed. The hoglets were shuffling around their pen, bumping into one another. Mr Hope pointed to a tray laid out with syringes. "The hoglets need feeding every two hours," he said. "Can I put you two in charge of that for the next two feeds? Mrs Hope and I are going to be very busy with Caturday."

Amelia felt a rush of pride at being asked to do something so important. "No problem," she said.

Mr Hope smiled. "I knew we could count on you." He explained the correct measures of kitten formula and wrote them on a pad next to the syringes. Then he left them to it.

The hoglets accepted the syringes straight away, and soon they were well fed and sleepy. Amelia held the smallest one in her lap a bit longer. "He already looks better," she said, noticing that his nose was now a shiny black and doing lots of inquisitive twitching. "He's so cute. I don't want to put him down!"

Sam put the other two hoglets back in their pen. "While you're giving your hedgehog an extra cuddle, I'll say hello

to the cats." He reached inside the pen to say hello to the mother cat and her baby. Amelia heard the sound of contented purring, but then shouting in the distance drowned it out.

"What's going on?" Amelia said.

"It's coming from the reception area," said Sam. "It sounds like someone needs help!"

Amelia quickly put her hoglet back in the pen, then she and Sam hurried out.

In the reception area, the lady from the safari park had stopped in the middle of her talk. Everybody had turned to stare at someone else.

Tarik!

He was standing
in the doorway,
looking flustered and
upset. "It's my cat,
Pumpkin," he said,
his voice cracking.
"He's gone missing!
I'm scared he's hurt.
Has anyone brought him in?"

"I'm sorry, Tarik," Mrs Hope said. "We
haven't seen Pumpkin. When did he go
missing?"

"Last night. I've searched everywhere
for him!" Tarik looked around at the
audience. "Has anyone seen him? He's
ginger. He has a zigzag scar on his nose."

People in the audience shook their heads.

Amelia whispered to Sam, "So *that's* why Tarik wasn't here."

Sam nodded. "He must be really worried. I know I was, when Mac got lost that time."

Amelia knew what she had to do. *Tarik annoys me sometimes, but that doesn't matter now ... Pumpkin could be in trouble!*

Amelia and Sam hurried over to Tarik. "Sam and I will help you look for Pumpkin," she offered.

Tarik gave her a weak smile. "But you'll miss Dr Lo's talk ..."

"That's all right," said Amelia. "Pumpkin

is more important. Let's go!"

When they were nearly at Tarik's house, Amelia saw Ellie skipping in her front garden. She hurried over to her. "Have you seen Pumpkin? He's missing."

Ellie glanced up at Tarik and Sam, waiting by the gate. "No," she said. "But I'll help look for him."

"Are you sure?" asked Amelia. "After all, Pumpkin attacked Luna ..."

"Well, I'd hate it if Luna was missing," Ellie said. "Tarik must feel awful."

They joined the boys. When Tarik heard Ellie was going to help too, he smiled gratefully. "Thanks, Ellie."

Tarik let them into his house. "Mum!"

he called. "My friends have come to help me look for Pumpkin."

Tarik's mum came into the hall, still in her dressing gown. She yawned. "That's nice. Can you keep the noise down, though? Amina's finally fast asleep."

She doesn't seem very worried about Pumpkin, thought Amelia. *I suppose new babies are very tiring.*

They searched Tarik's whole house and garden, but there was no sign of Pumpkin. At last Sam whispered, "Amelia, we've searched everywhere. Pumpkin isn't here."

Amelia nodded. "We need to decide where to look next."

Tarik slumped down on a log in the garden. "We're never going to find him!" he groaned.

Amelia put a hand on his arm. "We won't give up."

"We'll search the whole village if we have to," Sam added.

Amelia thought hard. "Why don't we split up into pairs? We can cover more ground that way."

"Good idea," Ellie agreed quickly. "I'll go with Sam."

Amelia nodded. "But we'll need a

way to let the others know if we find Pumpkin …"

"I'll ask my mum if I can borrow her phone," said Ellie, climbing over the fence into her garden.

Tarik ran to the back door. "Dad!" he shouted into the house. "Can we borrow your mobile phone?"

Indoors, the baby started crying with a high, piercing wail.

"*WAAAAAHHHHH!!!*" Amelia winced and covered her ears.

"Tarik!" said his father, appearing at the door. "What have we told you

about shouting when the baby's asleep?"

Tarik groaned. "Sorry, Dad!" he said. "I forgot. I still can't find Pumpkin. Can I borrow your phone?"

"As long as you use it quietly!" said his father, taking his phone out of his pocket and handing it to Tarik.

Just then, Ellie came back over the fence, waving another mobile phone. "Got it!" She and Tarik exchanged numbers.

Amina was still crying, the sound carrying across the garden.

Sam winced. "Whoa! Babies really are noisy!"

"You know," Amelia said thoughtfully,

"Dr Lo said cats don't like change. A crying baby in the house is a really big change."

Sam's eyes widened. "Maybe big enough to make Pumpkin run away!"

They went out into the street. "I'll go that way with Ellie," said Sam, pointing to the left.

"And we'll go this way," said Tarik, pointing right. "Thanks for helping me out, guys."

Sam grinned. "Don't worry, Tarik. We've found lost animals before."

"We'll leave no stone unturned," added Amelia. "Come on – let's find Pumpkin!"

CHAPTER FOUR

Amelia and Tarik rushed around Welford, peering into every garden and asking everybody they met if they'd seen Pumpkin. Once, Amelia saw a ginger cat strolling along the lane. She gasped and grabbed Tarik's arm, but he shook his head. This cat had white paws and

no battle scars. Up close, it wasn't like Pumpkin at all!

They went round the back of the Indian takeaway and looked behind the bins.

Nothing!

They carried on to Welford village shop. Tarik showed the shop assistant a photo of Pumpkin on his dad's phone. The assistant shook her head. "I haven't seen him," she said, "but one of my customers might have. I'll ask everyone who comes in."

Tarik thanked her and they hurried back into the street to continue the search for Pumpkin.

They walked for miles. When at last
they came to the edge of the village,
the woods began. Amelia gazed into the
tangled thickets. "Do you think Pumpkin
would come this far?"

Tarik shook his head. "I doubt it."

Tarik's phone rang. He answered it
quickly. "Hi, Ellie. Have you found him?"
Tarik's shoulders sagged. "OK, see you
there."

"No luck?" asked Amelia.

Tarik shook his head. "We're going to
meet them back at Animal Ark." He let
out a deep sigh. "We're never going to
find Pumpkin!"

"Yes, we will," said Amelia. "Dr Lo

might be able to help. She'll have ideas about where a runaway cat would go."

They met up with Sam and Ellie outside Animal Ark and headed for the doors. Two teenage boys were going up the steps ahead of them. "I want to find out about cat fights," a boy in a baseball hat said to the other boy. "There was one outside last night and the yowling woke me up."

Amelia met Sam's startled eyes.

A clue!

She hurried forward. "Hi," she said, feeling shy because the boys were a lot older than her. *But we've got to find Pumpkin*, she told herself. Plucking up her courage, she said, "Did you say you heard a cat fight? Where was it? We're looking for a lost cat."

The boy shrugged. "It sounded like the noise was coming from the park. My house backs on to it."

"Thanks!" said Amelia. She turned to her friends. "Come on, guys. Let's go!"

Amelia and Tarik raced up the street, with Sam and Ellie close behind. A few minutes later they were in the park. It was a wide green, dotted with trees. There was a toddlers' playground in the middle, with a low wooden fence around the brightly coloured climbing frames, slides and swings.

They hopped over the fence into the playground and began to search. Suddenly, Tarik gasped. "Look!" He tugged at something caught in one of the fence posts. He held it up triumphantly to show them, a smile on his face. It was a tuft of ginger fur!

Amelia felt a surge of excitement. "Pumpkin might be here somewhere!" She perched on one of the swings and looked around, thinking hard. *Where would Pumpkin hide?*

Ellie bent down to peer under the roundabout. "He's not here."

Sam looked underneath the slide. "Nope – he's not hiding here."

Tarik disappeared into a colourful playhouse. He stuck his head out of the window and called, "He's not in here either!"

Amelia frowned. *There's only one place we haven't looked …*

The climbing frame was made of

wood and rope. Amelia hopped off the swing and scrambled up the rope ladder. It led to a little wooden hut. Ducking her head, Amelia climbed awkwardly through the small doorway.

It was gloomy in the hut, but Amelia spotted him straight away.

"Pumpkin!" she said softly. "There you are!" Tarik's cat was crouched in the corner, paws and head tucked in as if he was trying to make himself as small as possible.

Amelia stuck her head out of the little door. "Tarik! He's in here!"

Tarik came running and climbed up into the hut. Amelia moved aside to make room for him in the cramped space. She felt her eyes well up as he gently picked up his pet.

"Hello, Pumpkin," he whispered. "We've been looking everywhere for you!"

Pumpkin bumped his head under Tarik's chin and rubbed his owner's cheek with his own. He began to purr.

Sam and Ellie climbed up the rope ladder and peered in the doorway. "Well, he doesn't seem to be hurt!" said Sam.

Tarik hugged Pumpkin harder. "I'm so glad he's OK. Thank you, guys. I never would have found him without you!"

"We're just happy he's safe," said Amelia.

They all climbed down then crowded round to stroke Pumpkin. The big ginger cat kept nuzzling Tarik's face and purring.

"He's so friendly now," said Amelia. "You were right, Tarik. In the garden, he was just defending his territory."

Tarik nodded. "I'm sure once he's used to Luna being around he'll stop thinking he owns Ellie's garden. Then I expect they'll get on better. Maybe they'll even become friends."

His words made Amelia's tummy feel funny.

Pumpkin isn't the only one being territorial, she thought. *I've been acting as if I own Animal Ark!*

"Um," she said. "I'm sorry, Tarik. I haven't been very nice. I shouldn't have got annoyed with you for helping with Caturday. It was a really nice thing to do."

Tarik smiled at her over Pumpkin's head. "That's OK. I love Animal Ark too."

"Animal Ark!" said Sam, his eyes widened. "What time do we have to feed the hoglets for Mr Hope?"

Amelia glanced at her watch. "Five minutes ago! Oh no!"

Tarik and Ellie looked confused. "What are you talking about?" asked Ellie.

"We'll tell you later!" Amelia called over her shoulder as she and Sam started to run. "See you at Animal Ark!"

The surgery was still full of people listening to Dr Lo's Caturday talk. Everyone turned to stare at Amelia and Sam as they burst through the door. Amelia saw Mrs Hope's startled face as she rushed past, but there wasn't time to stop and explain.

They dashed into the residential unit. Amelia heard Sam gasp, and her heart plummeted. The hedgehogs' pen was completely empty!

"They must have escaped somehow," said Sam. "But where have they gone?"

Amelia felt a lump in her throat. She knew that the poor little hoglets wouldn't last very long on their own. *We have to find them!*

CHAPTER FIVE

Amelia looked around the "hotel" desperately and saw that the door to the mother cat's pen was hanging open.

"Someone must have forgotten to latch this," she said. She went over to shut it and then she froze. Her heart did a somersault of joy. She couldn't believe her eyes. "Sam, look!" she whispered.

The mother cat was inside the pen. She was feeding not just her kitten, but the three hoglets too!

"Well I never," said Mrs Hope, coming in behind them. "The hedgehogs have got a new mum!"

Amelia tiptoed forward, with the others close behind. They crowded around the pen and stared in amazement.

"Whoa!" said Sam. "I guess the cat got out and lifted the hoglets out of their pen."

"I didn't expect that," Mrs Hope said. "And I've seen some very curious things!"

Amelia let out her breath in a long sigh. "It's the cutest thing ever!"

The little black kitten snuggled between her spiny new siblings. Purring contentedly, the mother cat licked a hoglet, smoothing down his spines just as if they were soft kitten fur.

Amelia gazed at the strange little family, enchanted. When the door swung open behind her it made her jump.

Mr Hope came in with another man.

"Everything OK in here?" he asked. "Mr Hyde has come to see Misty and her kitten."

Mrs Hope chuckled. "Come and look, Mr Hyde. You'll never believe it!"

Mr Hyde stared into the pen. His eyes widened and he leaned closer. "Goodness gracious!" He scratched his head and a slow smile spread over his face. "Does this happen often?"

"I've heard of mother cats feeding babies of other species," said Mr Hope.

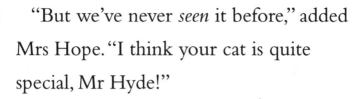

"But we've never *seen* it before," added Mrs Hope. "I think your cat is quite special, Mr Hyde!"

"I agree," Mr Hyde said. "I can't wait to get Misty home. I'll take her as soon as you think she's well enough. And if it's all right with you, I'll take *all* her new babies, too. Then she can carry on looking after them."

"Have you got a good garden for hedgehogs?" Amelia asked.

Mr Hyde smiled down at her. "Oh, yes. It's nice and big, with lots of hiding places. There are already holes in the fences to let wildlife wander in and out. We call them hedgehog highways. I'll add a couple of shelters in the garden. Hopefully the hedgehogs will stick around when they're older and eat some of my garden snails!"

Amelia nodded, satisfied. She looked around and saw that everyone was smiling broadly.

Mrs Hope carefully closed the pen, and they all trooped back to the waiting room to catch the end of Dr Lo's talk. Amelia and Sam squeezed in at the back

next to Tarik and Ellie. A smartly dressed woman was asking how to stop her cat clawing at the furniture.

"A scratching post should help," Dr Lo told the lady. "Maybe put some food on top to entice your cat. Or tie a toy to it. Your cat will soon get the message."

"How's Pumpkin?" whispered Sam.

"Safely back at home," Tarik whispered back. "I guess it'll take him time to get used to the new baby."

"Tarik," Amelia whispered. "You should ask Dr Lo about Pumpkin!"

To Amelia's surprise, Tarik looked shy. "Go on," she urged him.

Tarik put up his hand, and when Dr Lo turned to him with a smile, he asked his question a little nervously. "I've got a new baby sister. My cat, Pumpkin, er … doesn't like her crying. What should I do?"

"Excellent question!" said Dr Lo.

"Congratulations on the new baby in your family. Pumpkin will adjust, but it will take a little time. In the meantime, give him lots of love and attention whenever the baby is around. That will make him associate her with nice things."

Tarik nodded.

"Also," Dr Lo went on, "ask your parents to keep a quiet place in the house where the baby doesn't go. Maybe the utility room, or your bedroom."

Tarik nodded again. "The utility room might work. I can hear the baby crying through my bedroom wall! It was hard to sleep last night." He sat back down and grinned at Amelia.

Amelia was glad to see him smiling but she was worried too. It sounded like Pumpkin wasn't the only one struggling with having a new baby in the house. Tarik's whole life had been turned upside down by his little sister's arrival. No wonder he'd wanted to spend so much time helping at the vet's …

When there were no more questions for Dr Lo, Mrs Hope stood up. "Well, that's the last of our Caturday sessions. We hope you've all enjoyed the day. Thank you so much for coming. And a special thank you to Amelia Haywood, who came up with the idea for Caturday, and to her friends, Sam and Tarik, for all

162

their help. Stand up, guys."

Everybody clapped, and Amelia felt a warm blush on her cheeks.

I wish every Saturday could be a Caturday!

CHAPTER SIX

Everyone began to file out of Animal Ark, chattering about their cats and what they'd learned. Amelia noticed Tarik was looking a little sad as he helped her and Sam clear up.

"Are you OK?" she asked him quietly.

"I'm fine!" he said, smiling weakly as

he untacked a poster from the wall. "I'm just sad Caturday's over. It was really fun."

"I've got an idea," Amelia said. "Let's have a sleepover at mine tonight. Are you in, Sam?"

Sam nodded enthusiastically.

"What do you say, Tarik?" said Amelia.

Now Tarik beamed with real delight. "Really?"

"Of course! You might even get a good night's sleep away from your sister's crying. Though Sam does snore!"

"Hey!" said Sam, playfully punching Amelia's arm.

"That would be awesome," said Tarik.

"Great," said Amelia. "Maybe we can have a midnight feast!"

Tarik brought delicious freshly baked cupcakes, which they ate on a blanket in Amelia's room. But it wasn't anywhere close to midnight. By nine o'clock everyone was yawning so they crawled into their sleeping bags. As they lay there, with Star curled up next to them, Amelia and Sam told Tarik about all the amazing things they'd seen at Animal Ark. She thought he was listening quietly until she looked over and saw that Tarik was already fast asleep.

"I'm tired too. It's been such a busy day!" she said, switching off the light. "Night, Sam."

"Happy Caturday," he replied.

The next morning, as they headed downstairs for breakfast, Star wound herself around Amelia's ankles. Amelia suddenly remembered what day it was.

"Star's allowed to go outside for the first time today!"

Amelia and her friends ran through the kitchen, dashing past Mum and Gran. Star seemed to understand something important was happening, because she trotted after them.

"Morning all," said Gran. "Don't you want to have something to eat before you go outside?"

"Breakfast can wait!" said Amelia.

Sam rubbed his stomach. "I'm still full from all the cakes we ate last night!"

With Tarik and Sam watching, Amelia opened the back door. Star looked up at her and gave a questioning meow.

"It's all right, Star. We're going out with you," said Amelia.

They put on their shoes and stepped outside. The kitten stood on the threshold and rubbed her cheek against the doorframe.

"She's thinking about it," said Sam.

Amelia held her breath. Star put out one paw and then another. She stood in the doorway for a moment, half in and half out. The breeze ruffled the black and ginger markings on her fur. The kitten blinked and lifted her face to the light. Then she stepped all the way out.

"Way to go, Star!" said Tarik, offering Amelia a high five.

Star took her time exploring. She
sniffed the coconut doormat, treading
the surface gingerly as she felt the
prickles under her feet. Then she
stepped off it, on to the path. A blackbird
began to sing and Star's ears swivelled,
following the sound. She tiptoed on to
the grass, sniffing the dew-covered blades

one at a time. She looked back at Amelia for reassurance.

"Go on, Star," said Amelia encouragingly. "You're doing great."

Suddenly there was a blur of grey stripes and Luna appeared, balanced on top of the fence.

Amelia drew in her breath. "Uh-oh!"

"This could mean trouble!" said Sam, frowning.

Luna watched Star for a few minutes, then she jumped down on to the grass and began to lope across the garden.

Amelia watched her carefully. "She thinks this is her territory."

Tarik looked worried. "I hope Luna hasn't learned bad habits from Pumpkin!"

Amelia's fingers itched to pick Star up and protect her, but she managed to resist. Ellie's cat stalked towards Star. Curious, Star went over to meet her.

Luna blinked slowly. Star blinked back.
Luna nudged Star's face with hers. Star
nudged her back.

Suddenly the two kittens were sniffing
and nuzzling each other all over. Star
swiped at Luna's tail with a soft paw, and
Luna playfully batted her back. Then the

kittens began to frolic together.

Sam let out a sigh of relief. "I think Star's made a new friend."

Amelia looked sideways at Tarik, who was smiling as he watched the kittens play. *And so have I!* she thought, with a happy grin.

The End

Read on for a sneak peek at
Amelia and Sam's next adventure!

Doggy Drama

Lucy Daniels

A young woman with short hair tucked
behind her ears came into the surgery.
She was carrying an animal wrapped
in a blanket. A furry brown tail peeked
through the folds.

"Hi, Miss Sachs!" said Sam.

Amelia realised it was their drama
club teacher from school. Tucked in the
blanket, a cute little brown Yorkshire
Terrier gazed back at them with big
eyes. A cast covered one of his front legs.

"Oh no!" said Amelia. "What
happened?"

"He was trying to swim," said Miss
Sachs. She sighed and rubbed the

puppy's ears. "Oscar can't resist playing in the water. He jumped into a river but the water was too shallow. His leg broke when he hit the bottom. Luckily, he's having his cast taken off today."

Mrs Hope called Miss Sachs and Oscar into the treatment room. "You two can come and help," she said to Amelia and Sam.

They shared an excited smile, and followed Miss Sachs and the patient.

In the treatment room, Mrs Hope lifted Oscar onto the examining table. Sam stroked him gently to keep him calm, while Amelia held his leg still for Mrs Hope. Carefully, she cut the cast off with a large pair of scissors. Oscar yawned and licked his lips nervously, but he didn't flinch.

What a good dog, thought Amelia.

Mrs Hope unwrapped the bandage and padding that was underneath the cast, then felt along Oscar's leg. Amelia watched intently.

"It feels like the break has healed," said Mrs Hope. "What do you think, little guy? Do you want to try walking on it?"

Gently, she put Oscar on the floor. Amelia held her breath. Oscar lifted his bad leg off the floor and hobbled along on his three good legs. He stopped and his tail drooped dejectedly.

"Go on, Oscar," Miss Sachs encouraged him.

But the dog just lay down at her feet. He sniffed at the newly exposed leg and licked the fur.

"Poor Oscar," said Amelia. "He's not feeling very playful."

"I guess he's not ready to put any weight on it yet," said Mrs Hope. "It will take some time for him to get back to normal. In the meantime, he'll need some light exercise, along with lots of extra love and attention."

"Oh dear." Miss Sachs frowned. "The school play is coming up and I haven't got much time right now."

Amelia exchanged a glance with Sam. Last week they'd auditioned for parts in the school play, but with all the excitement of becoming a helper at Animal Ark, Amelia had forgotten about it.

"My usual dog walker takes Oscar out with a group of dogs, so he can't give him any extra attention," Miss Sachs continued. "What am I going to do?"

Amelia leaned over and stroked Oscar's smooth, silky fur. "I wish there was something I could do to help," she murmured, as the dog nuzzled his soft, warm nose into her hand.

"Me too!" added Sam.

Miss Sachs wrapped the dog up in the blanket again and carried him to the door. "I'll see you two at drama club," she called to Amelia and Sam.

After Miss Sachs and Oscar had left, Mrs Hope said, "So you two are budding actors as well as vets."

"We're doing *The Wizard of Oz*," Sam told her. "I want to be the Tin Man."

"I auditioned to be Dorothy," said Amelia.

"And is Mac going to be Dorothy's dog Toto?" asked Mrs Hope.

"I hope so!" said Sam. "He'd be great on stage. He's really well-behaved now.

Most of the time, anyway."

Talking about the play reminded Amelia that they still had a whole day of school ahead of them. She looked at her watch. "Sam, we'd better go or we'll be late!"

"Well, thanks for all your help!" said Mrs Hope. "See you again tomorrow morning!"

"Obviously Miss Sachs will pick me be Dorothy," Tiffany declared after school. "I'm going to be a famous actress when I grow up."

Sam rolled his eyes and Amelia bit her

lip to stifled a giggle.

The drama club was in the classroom waiting for Miss Sachs to come and announce the cast for *The Wizard of Oz*.

"And Sparkle will make the perfect Toto," Tiffany continued. "He's so clever. He can roll over, sit up and beg, and even fetch my headphones." Sparkle was Tiffany's bichon frise – a fluffy white puppy, who she usually carried around in a special backpack.

Just then, Miss Sachs arrived, followed by Oscar on his lead. The tiny terrier was still hobbling on three legs.

Amelia knelt down next to him. "Hello, Oscar. Remember me?"

His tail wagged as he licked her hand. *If only I could help you get better,* thought Amelia.

"Gather round, everyone," said Miss Sachs. She held up a clipboard. "I've got the cast list here."

Immediately, everyone was quiet. Amelia's heart beat faster.

"I'm afraid you can't all have the part you want," Miss Sachs continued. "Otherwise, we'd have seven Dorothys! But you're all important to the success of the play, no matter which role you have."

She looked at her list. "The role of the Cowardly Lion goes to Caleb. Karel, I've chosen you to be the Tin Man."

Amelia glanced over at Sam. He looked disappointed.

"Sam, I think you'll make an excellent Scarecrow," said Miss Sachs.

"Cool!" Sam's face immediately lit up, his brown eyes sparkling.

"Izzy, you've got the part of Glinda the Good Witch," Miss Sachs went on.

Amelia saw her friend clap her hands with glee.

"And Tiffany," said Miss Sachs, "with your dramatic talent, I think you'll be perfect for—"

"Dorothy!" Tiffany shouted. "I'm Dorothy!"

"Actually," said Miss Sachs, "you're going to be the Wicked Witch of the West."

"But who's playing Dorothy?" wailed Tiffany.

Miss Sachs looked at her clipboard. "Well, I had a tough choice, especially as so many of you tried out to be Dorothy. But I've decided to cast Amelia because she did such a great audition."

Me? Amelia wasn't sure she'd heard correctly.

"Well done, Amelia!" said Sam.

Amelia blushed, especially when her friends gathered round to congratulate her. But she spotted Tiffany glaring at her from the other side of the room.

"Miss Sachs, who's going to be Toto?" asked Sam.

Miss Sachs smiled. "Well, I've heard your dog Mac is very well trained, so it makes sense for him to take the role. Toto is supposed to be a terrier, after all."

Everyone erupted into cheers – all except for Tiffany, who was dabbing her eyes with a tissue...

Read **Doggy Drama** to find out
what happens next ...

Animal Advice

Do you love animals as much as Amelia and Sam? Here are some tips on how to look after them from veterinary surgeon Sarah McGurk.

Caring for your pet

1 Animals need clean water at all times.

2 They need to be fed too – ask your vet what kind of food is best, and how much the animal needs.

3 Some animals, such as dogs, need exercise every day.

4 Animals also need lots of love. You should always be very gentle with your pets and be careful not to do anything that might hurt them.

When to go to the vet

Sometimes animals get ill. Like you, they will mostly get better on their own. But if your pet has hurt itself or seems very unwell, then a trip to the vet might be needed. Some pets also need to be vaccinated, to prevent them from getting dangerous diseases. Your vet can tell you what your pet needs.

Helping wildlife

- Always ask an adult before you go near any animals you don't know.
- If you find an animal or bird which is injured or can't move, it is best not to touch it.
- If you are worried, you can phone an animal charity such as the RSPCA (SSPCA in Scotland) for help.